The Last of the Mohicans

Artist: Li Sidong

First edition for North America (including Canada and Mexico),
Philippine Islands, and Puerto Rico published in 2010
by Barron's Educational Series, Inc.

All inquiries should be addressed to:
Barron's Educational Series, Inc.
250 Wireless Blvd.
Hauppauge, NY 11788
www.barronseduc.com

ISBN-13 (Hardcover): 978-0-7641-6299-2
ISBN-10 (Hardcover): 0-7641-6299-3
ISBN-13 (Paperback): 978-0-7641-4447-9
ISBN-10 (Paperback): 0-7641-4447-2

Library of Congress Control No.: 2009930808

Picture credits:
p. 40 The Granger Collection / TopFoto / TopFoto.co.uk
p. 44 The Granger Collection / TopFoto / TopFoto.co.uk
p. 47 KPA / HIP / TopFoto / TopFoto.co.uk
Every effort has been made to trace copyright holders. The Salariya Book Company apologizes for
any omissions and would be pleased, in such cases, to add an acknowledgment in future editions.

Date of Manufacture: January 2010
Manufactured by: Leo Paper Products Ltd, Heshan, Guangdong, China

Printed and bound in China.
Printed on paper from sustainable sources.
9 8 7 6 5 4 3 2 1

The Last of the Mohicans

James Fenimore Cooper

Illustrated by

Li Sidong

BARRON'S

Retold by

Tom Ratliff

Series created and designed by

David Salariya

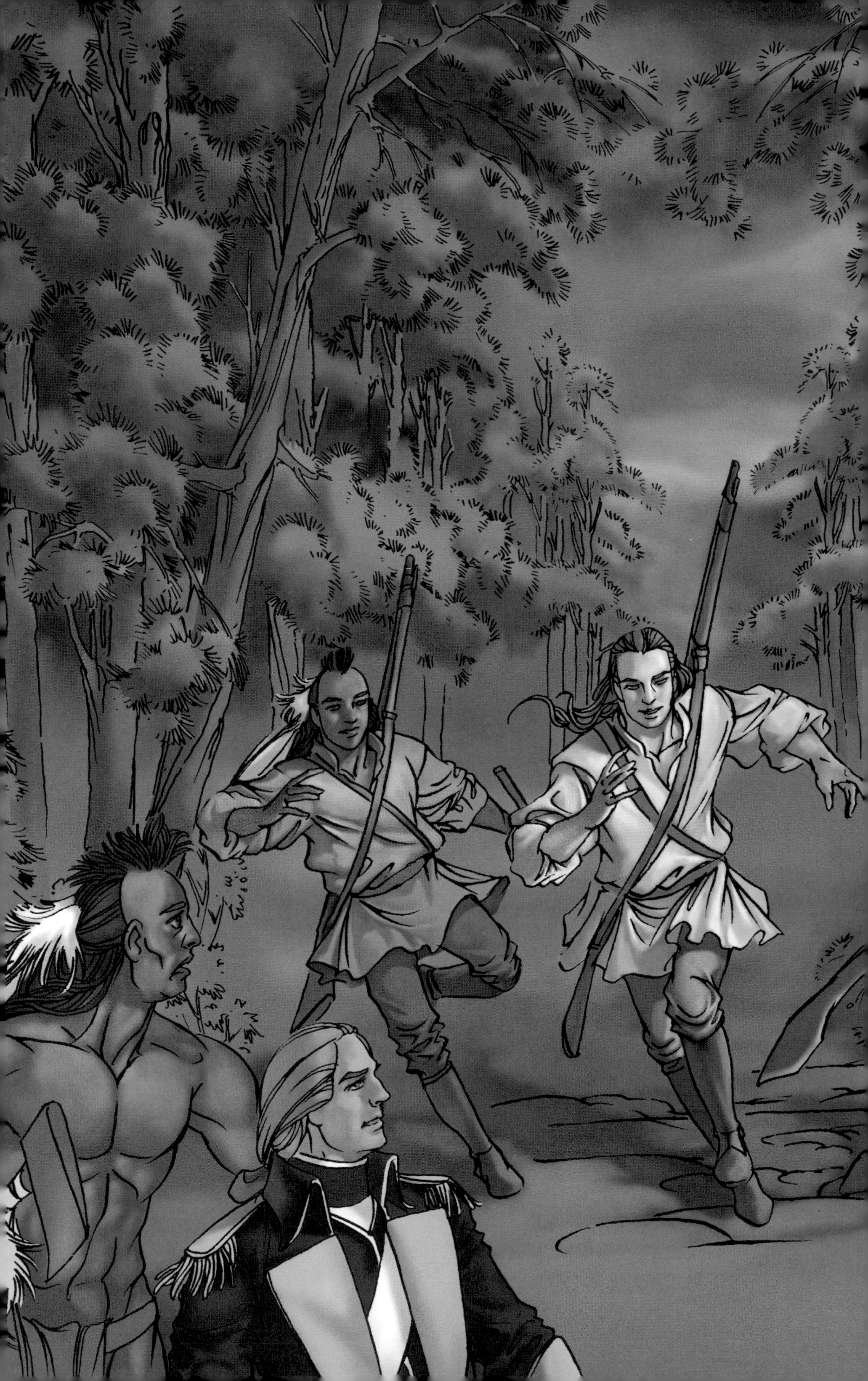

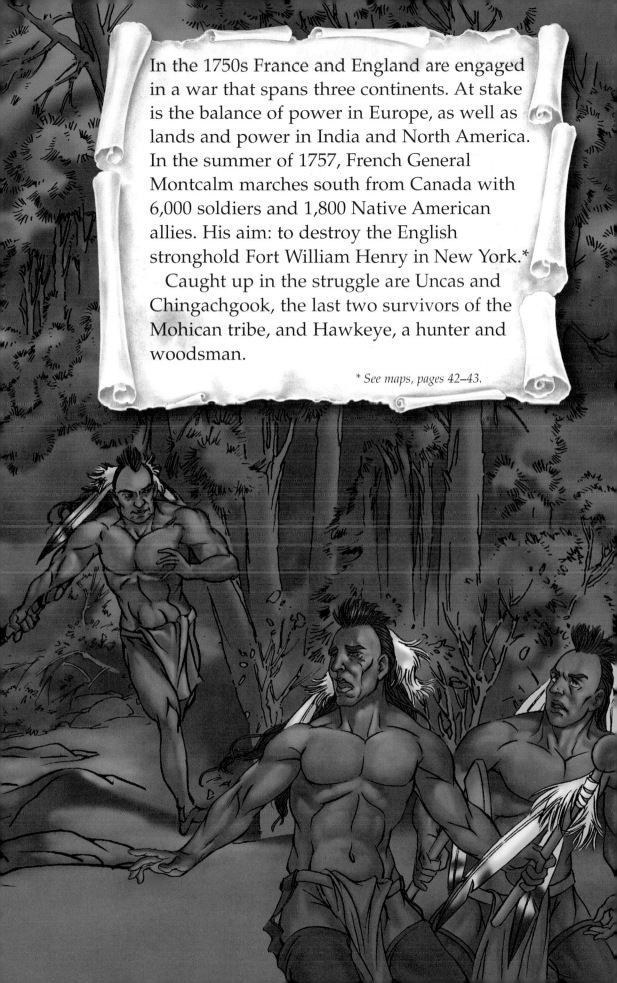

In the 1750s France and England are engaged in a war that spans three continents. At stake is the balance of power in Europe, as well as lands and power in India and North America. In the summer of 1757, French General Montcalm marches south from Canada with 6,000 soldiers and 1,800 Native American allies. His aim: to destroy the English stronghold Fort William Henry in New York.*

Caught up in the struggle are Uncas and Chingachgook, the last two survivors of the Mohican tribe, and Hawkeye, a hunter and woodsman.

* See maps, pages 42–43.

CHARACTERS

Chingachgook, chief of the Mohican tribe

Magua, or *Le Renard Subtil* (The Crafty Fox), of the Huron tribe

Tamenund, leader of the Delaware tribe

Hawkeye, or *La Longue Carabine* (The Long Rifle), a hunter and woodsman

Uncas, or *Le Cerf Agile* (The Bounding Elk), Chingachgook's son

Major Duncan Heyward of the British army

British Colonel Munro

French General Montcalm

David Gamut, preacher and singer of psalms

Cora, Colonel Munro's elder daughter

Alice, Colonel Munro's younger daughter

FORT EDWARD

Two English outposts[1] – Fort Edward, commanded by General Webb, and Fort William Henry, commanded by Colonel Munro – guard the northern boundary of the Hudson River Valley. The two forts are separated by a day's march. A large French army is coming to attack Fort William Henry.

Fort Edward, August 1757.

An Indian runner[2] brings news of the coming attack on Fort William Henry.

General Webb agrees to send 1,500 troops to help Colonel Munro defend Fort William Henry.

Also headed to William Henry are Colonel Munro's daughters.

Goodbye, Major Heyward. I know you will see Cora and Alice safely to their father.

It is a dangerous journey, but our Indian scout,[3] Magua, will guide us through the wilderness.

Major Duncan Heyward and his charges[4] follow the scout through the main gate.

In the shadows, an oddly dressed stranger takes careful note of their departure.

1. outposts: isolated forts.
2. runner: a messenger on foot.
3. scout: a guide.
4. charges: the people in Major Heyward's care.

THE WILDERNESS PATH

While the troops march north along the main road, the scout suggests a shortcut – a hidden path that will protect Munro's daughters from attack by the French or their Huron[1] allies.

Why do we leave the main road?

We take a secret path known only to our guide.

Should we mistrust the man because his manners are not ours[2] and his skin is dark?

What do you think of our scout, Cora? I like him not.

Magua silently leads them down a narrow track.

Suddenly the little party is overtaken by a stranger!

I am David Gamut, a singer of psalms.[3]

Who are you, sir?

It will be nice to have some music on our journey. I am glad to encounter thee,[4] friend.

We are not in need of psalms.

Do you have a weapon?

Only my pitch pipe,[5] which helps me to carry a tune.

"Oh how good it is, And how it pleases well, Together in our unity, Our brethren to dwell!"

As the day progresses, Duncan has an uneasy feeling that they are being watched.

1. Huron: a North American tribe (also known as Wyandotte) found in Canada and the Ohio River Valley; at this time, the Hurons were allied with the French army.   2. his manners are not ours: his behavior is not like ours.
3. psalm: a holy song – there are 150 featured in the Bible.
4. glad to encounter thee: glad to have met you.
5. pitch pipe: a musical instrument, similar to a recorder, used to provide a starting note for singers.

A few miles west, two men sit on the banks of a small stream, vast trees overhanging the water. The stream's vapors cool the drowsy heat of the July afternoon.

Chingachgook, the Mohicans[1] have disappeared from the forest.

Yes, Hawkeye. What the Mohawk[2] and the Mingo[3] could not do, the Dutch[4] accomplished with fire-water.[5]

And now the French invade these woods, too.

But the Hurons are the real enemy.

As long as I have Killdeer,[6] I fear no man.

What I fear is that my tribe is no more, for my son Uncas is the last of the Mohicans.

Who speaks of me?

How does the scouting go? Are there enemies nearby?

The French have spies everywhere.

Hssst! Someone approaches!

The horses of white men are coming.

Uncas silently emerges from the forest.

1. the Mohicans: a Native American tribe who once lived in western New England and the Hudson River Valley.   2. the Mohawk: a Native American tribe. They were traditional enemies of the Mohicans, as their tribal lands overlapped and each competed for control of the fur trade.   3. the Mingos: another Native American tribe, but Hawkeye uses the term "Mingo" to refer to any enemy tribe.   4. the Dutch: settlers from Holland whom Chingachgook blames for his tribe's downfall.   5. fire-water: alcohol.   6. Killdeer: Hawkeye's name for his rifle.

9

MAGUA'S TREACHERY

A band of riders appears.

Do you know the distance to Fort William Henry?

We left Fort Edward this morning headed for Fort William Henry.

You are as much off the scent as possible.

Follow the river back to Fort Edward and ask General Webb for a guide.

Then you have lost your eyesight — you should be on the portage road.[1]

We took this path on the advice of our Indian guide.

'Tis strange an Indian should be lost in the woods. Is he a Mohawk?

No, he is a Huron, but he has been adopted by the Mohawk tribe.

A Huron! A thievish race of skunks and vagabonds! What name does he go by?

His French name is *Le Renard Subtil*.[2]

Magua!

He has led them into a trap!

We must not let him get away!

Sensing danger, Magua has already fled.

BANG!

But Hawkeye manages to take a shot before the Huron disappears into the forest.

1. the portage road: the main road between the forts. "Portage" means a route connecting two waterways – in this case the Hudson River and Lake George.
2. *Le Renard Subtil*: French for "The Crafty Fox."

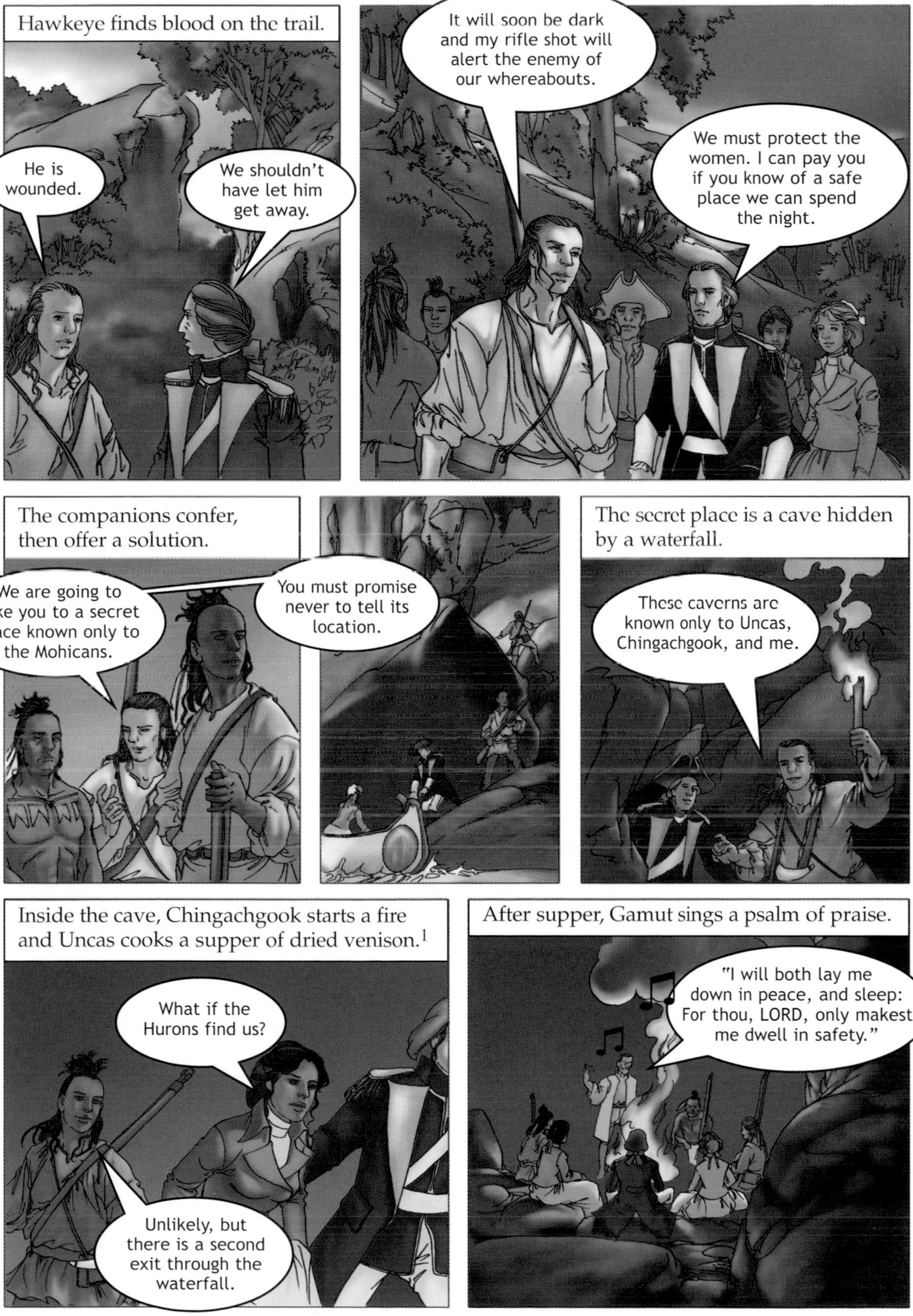
Hawkeye finds blood on the trail.
He is wounded.
We shouldn't have let him get away.
It will soon be dark and my rifle shot will alert the enemy of our whereabouts.
We must protect the women. I can pay you if you know of a safe place we can spend the night.
The companions confer, then offer a solution.
We are going to take you to a secret place known only to the Mohicans.
You must promise never to tell its location.
The secret place is a cave hidden by a waterfall.
These caverns are known only to Uncas, Chingachgook, and me.
Inside the cave, Chingachgook starts a fire and Uncas cooks a supper of dried venison.[1]
What if the Hurons find us?
Unlikely, but there is a second exit through the waterfall.
After supper, Gamut sings a psalm of praise.
"I will both lay me down in peace, and sleep: For thou, LORD, only makest me dwell in safety."

1. venison: deer meat.

NOISES IN THE NIGHT

While Duncan, Alice, and Cora sleep, Hawkeye and Uncas keep guard near the mouth of the cavern.

SHRIEEEK!

We must be alert. The Hurons are near.

The cry has awoken Duncan.

What was that sound?

It is nothing. Go back to sleep.

The hours pass but the horrid cry comes a second time!

What's making that sound?

It might be wolves.

The sky overhead hints at the coming morning.

It is almost first light.

Yes, we have a long journey back to Fort Edward.

As they prepare to leave, the Hurons attack!

We are discovered!

Hawkeye and Uncas take cover, but David Gamut is hit by a Huron bullet.

Argh!

Our main hope is to keep[1] the rock until Munro can send for help.

Hawkeye's aim is true, and Killdeer finds revenge for the wounded psalmist.

BANG!

Cora is worried about Gamut.

Is he dead?

No, his heart has life.

1. keep: defend.

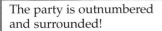

The party is outnumbered and surrounded!

There must be twenty or thirty of them!

With our rifles we can hold them off for a long time.

The Hurons float down the river in hope of a surprise attack.

But Hawkeye is not fooled.

Hssst! Freshen your prime![1]

Hawkeye and Uncas shoot two Hurons.

At the crucial moment, Duncan's pistols misfire![2]

Click!

Hawkeye's knife makes short work of the enemy.

But Duncan is not so lucky.

My sword!

SNAP!

Duncan and his Huron adversary[3] are caught in a deadly struggle.

Fortunately, Uncas comes to the rescue.

1. Freshen your prime: Put new gunpowder in your gun.
2. misfire: stop working.
3. adversary: enemy, attacker.

Escape and Capture

The battle continues through the morning.

Uncas saved my life.

Life is an obligation which friends owe each other[1] in the wilderness.

As Duncan peers over a rock, a bullet scrapes his shoulder.

Keep your head down or lose your hair![2]

BANG!

Hawkeye's keen sight finds a Huron who has climbed a tree across the river.

That's the last of my powder!

Mine too!

Without ammunition, the party is doomed.

We have fought our last battle.

Why die at all? Go, we owe you too much already.

Better a man to die than desert his friends.

But if you reach Fort Edward, perhaps we can be rescued.

Wisdom is sometimes given to the young.

Laying aside his long rifle, Hawkeye follows his Mohican companions into the river.

Go, Duncan — follow these wise men.

I made a promise to your father and I will not desert you.

14   1. Life . . . each other: It is our duty to protect one another.   2. lose your hair: many Native American tribes engaged in scalping – cutting off a tuft of hair from an enemy – in the belief that the scalp symbolized the life-force of a warrior.

Alice, Cora, Duncan, and David retreat into the back of the cavern.

Do you think we are safe?

We are not discovered, there is still hope.

La Longue Carabine![1]

Tense moments pass as the little party huddles in the dark. A shout announces that the Hurons are nearby.

They have found Hawkeye's rifle.

Now is the moment of our uncertainty . . . in two hours we may expect help from General Webb.

Suddenly light bursts into the cavern and a familiar face peers into the cave — it's Magua!

BANG!

Duncan reacts quickly, but Magua disappears. Hurons rush in – the party is captured.

Where is La Longue Carabine?

He that you call Long Rifle is gone.

And the Mohican dogs that accompany him?

They have escaped, too.

1. *La Longue Carabine*: French for "The Long Rifle" – the Hurons' name for Hawkeye.

Cora and Magua

The prisoners are bound and taken across the river.

Duncan tries to persuade Magua to help them.

If you help us escape, Colonel Munro will reward you.

While most of the Hurons head for Fort William Henry, Magua takes his prisoners north toward his village.

Munro is my enemy. I will have my revenge.

Cora secretly leaves a trail of signals.

She snaps twigs and purposely drops one of her gloves.

After several hours of travel over rough ground, Magua calls a halt.

The Hurons kill a deer and set up camp for the night.

Bring the dark-haired one to me.

Cora Munro has been summoned by Magua.

I was a Huron chief, but the fire-water given to me by the White Man turned me into a villain, and I was chased out of my tribe.

I became a Mohawk warrior. For a while I served your father, Munro, until I broke his rule and drank fire-water.

For this I was tied up and whipped. See the scars I hide.

If my father has done you this injustice, show that you can forgive, and let us go.

That would not satisfy my hatred!

What would you have?[1]

I will release your sister and the others if you agree to be my wife.

I would have my revenge on Munro if his daughter drew my water, tended my corn, and cooked my venison.

I would rather die than have my sister and father suffer knowing that I was a captive of such a monster!

CONDEMNED

In his rage, Magua begins shouting orders.

Seize the prisoners!

They mean to torture us!

Is your head too good for a Huron pillow?

I will pray for you.

Then die!

Another Huron prepares to kill Alice.

Duncan suddenly breaks the bonds that hold him.

But without a weapon, he does not stand a chance.

Just as a Huron strikes, a shot rings out! Duncan's attacker falls to the ground, dead.

18

Hawkeye, Chingachgook, and Uncas have arrived just in time!

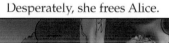

La Longue Carabine!

Chingachgook challenges Magua, and Duncan finds a weapon to fight with.

Exterminate the varlets![1]

Cora manages to break free, but is hurt.

Desperately, she frees Alice.

A Huron attacks Cora from behind, but Uncas leaps to her defense and stabs him in the back.

You are wounded!

It is not a deep cut.

Let him go — he is but one man.

Defeated, Magua pretends to give up, but escapes by rolling over the edge of a cliff.

1. varlets: unprincipled people.

THE TRAIL TO THE FORT

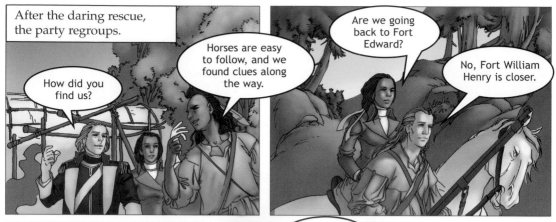

After the daring rescue, the party regroups.

How did you find us?

Horses are easy to follow, and we found clues along the way.

Are we going back to Fort Edward?

No, Fort William Henry is closer.

After dark, the trail is hard to see.

It is near midnight. Let us rest awhile.

Let me bind your wounds.

Chingachgook stands guard while his companions rest.

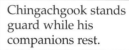

Before dawn, the little party sets off again.

By midmorning they reach a hilltop overlooking Fort William Henry. The fort is surrounded by French soldiers and Hurons, ready to attack.

We have a delicate needle to thread[1] here.

Their lines are impenetrable.[2]

Let us go to Montcalm and ask permission to enter the fort.

Montcalm would never consent to letting us cross his lines.

---

1. We have a delicate needle to thread: We have a difficult situation to get through.
2. impenetrable: impossible to get past.

A fog begins to roll in off nearby Lake George.

If the fog is thick enough, we can use it to sneak through the French lines.

As they approach, a French watchman calls out.

Qui vive?[1]

The quick-thinking Duncan responds.

Ami de la France.[2]

Through the fog the sally port[3] comes into view.

Hssst! Just a little farther.

But they do not reach the fort undetected!

BOOM!

Hawkeye, Uncas, and Chingachgook prepare to fight while the others run to safety.

The three men attack the French, helped by the English soldiers defending the fort.

BANG!

BANG!

Protected by fire from the fort, Hawkeye, and the Mohicans, the girls make it to safety.

Father!

1. *Qui vive?*: "Who goes there?"
2. *Ami de la France*: French for "A friend of France."
3. sally port: a gate through which soldiers can come out of the fort to attack.

SIEGE OF FORT WILLIAM HENRY

The French bombard the English with terrifying accuracy – the constant shelling is taking a toll on morale.[1] Munro talks to Duncan.

You are lucky to have made it through the French lines.

We were assisted by a man the Hurons call *La Longue Carabine*.

The fidelity[2] of the Long Rifle is well known to me.

Conditions have worsened since I left.

Half our cannon are burst[3] and our supplies run low.

Is General Webb sending more reinforcements?

Ha! Have ye looked to the south? Could ye not see them?[4]

General Montcalm wants to discuss our surrender.

Go to the French under a white flag.[5] It will give Webb more time to act.

As Duncan enters the French army's camp, he sees Magua among the soldiers.

1. taking a toll on morale: affecting the mood of the soldiers.
2. fidelity: loyalty.
3. burst: exploded by accident.
4. Ha! . . . see them?: Munro is bitterly disappointed that Webb has not sent more men to help fight against the French – his laugh is an angry one.
5. white flag: flag of truce.

22

Monsieur,[1] welcome to my camp. Are you here to surrender the fort?

Have you found our defense so feeble as to believe such a measure is necessary?

General Montcalm graciously welcomes the English officer.

I would be sorry if your defense brought irritation to my Huron allies.

If you continue to fight, I cannot guarantee your safety.

We expect to be reinforced any day now.

We have intercepted dispatches[2] from Fort Edward. Webb is not coming.

Only Colonel Munro can give the order to evacuate the fort.

Then we will send for him.

A short time later, Colonel Munro arrives.

Is it true? Has Webb refused to send more troops?

The man has betrayed me! He has brought dishonor and shame to my gray hairs!

Listen to my terms[4] before you depart.

You cannot frighten us with words.

Without Webb's help, Munro knows there's no hope of an English victory.

Let us go back and dig our graves behind the ramparts[3] of the fort.

To retain your command is impossible now. My orders are to destroy the fort, but there is no reason your army cannot march south as free men.

1. Monsieur: French for "Sir"; it also means "Mister" when placed before a person's name.
2. dispatches: messages.
3. ramparts: defensive walls.
4. terms: proposed rules.

THE FORT SURRENDERS

General Montcalm offers his surrender terms.

May we keep our flag?

Yes, monsieur.

And our weapons?

Unloaded, of course, but yes.

And our surrender?

Shall be honorable. My troops will stand aside and let you march out freely.

I have lived to see two things that I never did expect to behold:[1]

an Englishman afraid to support a friend, and a Frenchman too honest to profit from his advantage.[2]

August 9, 1757. The night is peaceful.

It is good to have a night of rest at last.

In the French camp, Montcalm and Magua have unfinished business.

White men make friends,

and Hurons have no scalps.

Our goal was to destroy the fort. Send your people home.

We were promised plunder[3] for our alliance.

I gave my word that the English can leave in peace.

Le Renard Subtil did not give *his* word.

1. behold: experience, see.
2. profit . . . advantage: Montcalm is kindly letting them leave, without taking advantage of the situation.
3. plunder: treasure.

24

August 10, 1757 – early morning. The British prepare to evacuate Fort William Henry.

Stay alert, men. Remember you are English soldiers!

The enemy watch as the English depart.

The English troops begin marching. Behind them come civilians and the wounded.

This place is no longer fit for the children of an English officer.

In the rear of the company walk the daughters of Munro.

God help us if the French don't keep their word.

A few Huron warriors approach the stragglers.

When the soldiers have passed by, Magua shouts the order to attack.

Leave us be, you heathen![1]

With no ammunition, the English are defenseless – the Hurons slaughter them.

Magua drags Cora away.

Never!

Come to the wigwam[2] of a Huron!

Alice and David Gamut pursue them.

1. heathen: a person of a different religion or no religion – meant to imply they are barbarians.
2. wigwam: a domed, often round shelter made of bent wood and covered with bark, moss, or animal skins.

THE SEARCHERS

Three days later, Fort William Henry is a smoldering ruin. The bodies of the dead lie in the fields, and the French and Huron enemy have departed.

My children! We must find them.

Montcalm will pay for this — his army did nothing to stop the slaughter.

This is the hand of the devil, plainly.

Uncas and Chingachgook search for evidence of the girls' whereabouts.

Have faith. Indian eyes can see the trail of a hummingbird.

It will be impossible to find any trace of them.

After much careful searching, Chingachgook finds a moccasin[1] print and horseshoe tracks.

This is the moccasin print of *Le Renard Subtil*.

Magua is taking them to his village in Canada.

The girls are alive!

Since Magua has a head start, it is decided to follow the lake as far north as they can.

Be careful to leave no tracks in the mud — there may be Huron scouts about.

We can travel faster by canoe.

Hssst! We must be vigilant.[2] Ours is a dangerous mission.

But there is trouble ahead . . .

Hurons!

Chingachgook has spotted smoke rising from an island in the lake.

26   1. moccasin: a shoe made of deerskin or other soft leather, worn by Native Americans and woodsmen like Hawkeye.
2. vigilant: alert.

What shall we do?

They haven't seen us — let's hope we slip past unnoticed.

The next several minutes pass in silence.

A little farther and we'll be out of the whistle of a bullet.[1]

A second later the quiet of the lake is pierced by a rifle shot.

BANG!

The Hurons may think they are out of range, but they have never seen a barrel[2] that matches Killdeer's.

Hawkeye reaches for his gun, but a Huron canoe appears from another direction.

Let us make for shore!

Hawkeye fires and kills two Hurons in the approaching canoe.

La Longue Carabine!

As the Hurons give up the chase, the men make it safely to shore.

The Hurons will not follow us for fear of the Long Rifle.

They move inland, and the Mohicans search for Magua's trail.

They camped here a few days ago.

Hawkeye finds Gamut's pitch pipe.

1. out of . . . bullet: out of the range of the enemy's gunfire.
2. barrel: the long, tubelike part of a gun.

THE CAPTIVE

Guided by the Mohicans, the search party follows Magua's trail north.

We must be careful.

We are nearing the Huron camp.

After several hours they reach a beaver meadow.[1]

Suddenly a solitary figure appears on a distant hill.

Can you shoot him from here?

Hssst! I will take him alive.

Hawkeye sneaks up on the stranger with knife drawn.

Hawkeye is amazed to discover the "Indian" is really Gamut!

The girls are safe. Alice is being held in the Huron village.

It is a happy reunion.

What about Cora?

Magua took her to another village, not far from here.

Why didn't you escape and bring the news?

It was my duty to stay and protect the girls from harm.

1. beaver meadow: a large pond with dozens of beaver lodges and several trees cut down or gnawed by beavers.

What tribe is Cora with?

I don't know.

Yes.

Do they paint themselves with the serpent?

Delaware![1]

How can we rescue my daughters?

Uncas and I will go to the Delaware and seek Cora's release.

Duncan forms a desperate plan to rescue Alice.

I will paint your face to disguise you.[2]

Since I speak French, I can pretend to be a French doctor sent to help the Hurons.

If the Hurons lift your scalp, Uncas and I will avenge your death.

The Hurons will recognize you as a friend.

With Munro and Chingachgook staying behind at the beaver meadow, the good-byes are hasty.

Hawkeye has a gift for the psalmist – Gamut's pitch pipe, found on the trail.

I was going to use this as firewood, but you might find it more useful.

With David Gamut as his guide, Duncan heads for the Huron village.

I come from General Montcalm.

Is the French father angry with the Hurons for taking revenge on the Yengeese?[3]

Montcalm is grateful to the mighty Hurons for slaying his enemies.

The Hurons are surprised to see a stranger in the wilderness.

Although appalled by his own words, Duncan is able to assure the Hurons he comes as a friend.

1. Delaware: An Eastern Indian tribe related to the Mohicans.
2. paint your face . . . you: It was common for French and English settlers to decorate their faces like their allied tribes to help Native Americans identify them as friends.
3. Yengeese: English settlers – in this case the settlers at Fort William Henry.

THE HURON VILLAGE

As a messenger from Montcalm, Duncan is invited to sit with the men in their lodge.

Duncan spends the afternoon searching the village for Alice.

To his dismay, he cannot find any trace of her.

Late in the day, shrill cries announce the return of a hunting party.

We have captured *Le Cerf Agile!*[1]

We will capture your friend, too.

Have you no ears? Two Hurons chased the Long Rifle and two shots rang out.[2]

In the morning we will see if you are still brave when we torture you.

As night falls Duncan tries again to search for Alice. But he is stopped by a tribal elder.[3]

My son's wife is possessed by evil spirits. Can you cure her?

I . . . I . . . why, yes.

She is in a cave near the village.

Duncan reluctantly follows the elder out of the camp.

The shaman has failed to drive out the evil spirit.

This could be dangerous.

As they approach the cave, they pass the tribal shaman,[4] dressed as a bear.

The evil spirit is powerful. Be careful.

Duncan is relieved that the tribal elder is too afraid to enter the cave.

---

1. *Le Cerf Agile*: Uncas is also known as *Le Cerf Agile,* or Bounding Elk, to the Hurons.   2. Have you . . . rang out: Did you not listen? Hawkeye fired two shots at the Hurons chasing him – he killed them.   3. tribal elder: a senior, respected tribesman.   4. shaman: a person who uses magic to cure or help people.

The cave is actually a series of caverns. Duncan finds the young woman in one of the small chambers.

This poor woman is already dead!

Duncan hears a noise behind him. The shaman has followed him into the cave!

Hssst!

Duncan soon realizes the shaman is really Hawkeye!

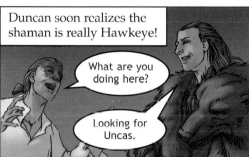

What are you doing here?

Looking for Uncas.

How did you get the shaman's costume?

I rapped the real shaman over the head on the outskirts of the village.

I haven't found Alice yet.

I think there is a prisoner in the next chamber.

Duncan enters another chamber.

Alice! Alice, it is me, Duncan.

I knew you would never desert me!

But the happy reunion is interrupted by an old adversary.

Magua! Do your worst — I am ready to die for Alice.

Will you speak these words when tied to the burning stake?

THE SHAMAN AND THE PSALMIST

Once again, Hawkeye comes to the rescue.

WHACK!

That ought to keep him out of the way until we can escape.

Poor Alice is too weak to walk far in the wilderness.

Where can we find safety?

The Delaware village is not far. Seek refuge there.

Aren't you coming with us?

The Hurons hold the last of the high blood[1] of the Mohicans. If I can't rescue Uncas, I will die for him.

Disguised as the tribal shaman, Hawkeye is able to move freely about the Huron village.

He encounters Gamut in one of the lodges.

What art thou?[2]

Put up the tootin' weapon[3] and listen.

Hawkeye fills Gamut in on the escape of Alice and Duncan.

And now, I've got to find Uncas.

That will not be difficult. The young man is near.

David Gamut leads Hawkeye to the lodge where Uncas is being held captive.

The shaman wants to see the miserable prisoner.

Hssst!

1. high blood: blood of the chiefs (who are like royalty) – Uncas is the son of the last Mohican chief.
2. What art thou?: What are you?
3. tootin' weapon: pitch pipe.

We have no weapons. How can we escape?

The psalmist and I have a plan.

By swapping clothes, we ought to be able to escape in the dark.

Hawkeye dresses in Gamut's clothes.

Are you sure you want to stay?

Uncas has battled on my behalf and I will help him escape.

You are a brave man, David Gamut.

The Hurons respect my singing. They will not harm me.

The guards are tired and don't pay any attention as Hawkeye and Uncas slip past.

But soon the deception is discovered.

Le Cerf Agile has escaped!

Magua has escaped from the cave. He is thirsty for revenge!

Their only hope is the Delaware tribe. We will catch them!

Le Cerf Agile!

La Longue Carabine!

THE DELAWARE VILLAGE

The Delaware village is peaceful as the sun comes up on a new day.

A familiar figure enters the village.

Does my prisoner give trouble?

She is welcome here.

And are there strange moccasin tracks in your village?

What do you mean?

Yengeese. I followed their trail here.

The Delaware village is always open to those who seek refuge.

If my greatest enemy is here in your camp, then who is my friend?

Who is it you speak of?

La Longue Carabine!

La Longue Carabine is here?

At the mention of Long Rifle, the village elders become alarmed.

The commotion is interrupted by the appearance of the tribal leader, Tamenund.

Bring the Yengeese to me. We shall see if *Le Renard* is correct.

Alice, Cora, Ducan, and Hawkeye are being held prisoner in the camp.

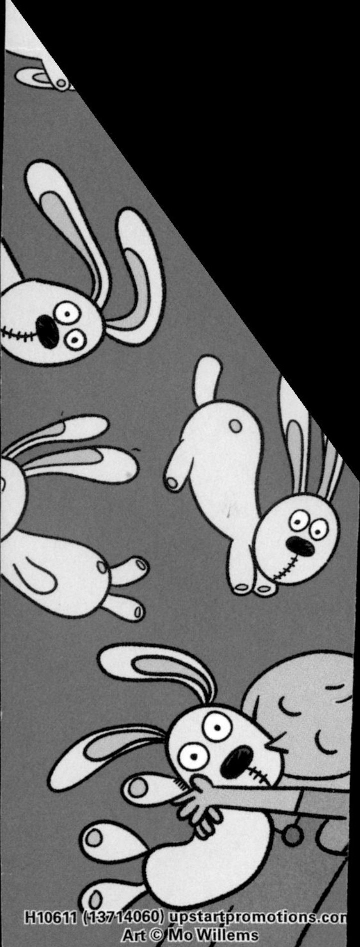

Which of you is *La Longue Carabine*?

I am!

No, it is the other!

Duncan and Hawkeye are asked to shoot at a target.

There is but one way to settle this.

Even with his hands tied, Hawkeye's aim is perfect.

He is the true *La Longue Carabine*.

Delaware! Listen to me! I am a friend of your people![1]

Don't listen to the lying Yengee.

Why has the Huron come?

To claim my prisoners.

Tribal law says we must honor the Huron's claim.

Oh, wise elder. Are you a father? Would you want your children returned to you?

I am father of a nation and must follow the law.

There is one more prisoner — let him speak!

The fifth prisoner appears – it's Uncas.

1. Delaware . . . people!: Hawkeye says this in the Delaware language.

The Mohican

What tongue[1] do you speak?

Like my fathers — the Delaware.

But you sneak into our camp like an enemy and must endure trial by fire.[2]

Oh, great chief. Have mercy on this young man!

A tribal elder grabs Uncas and rips off his shirt.

Who are you with the mark of the Great Tortoise?

I am Uncas, son of Chingachgook, son of Unamis — the Great Turtle.[3]

Uncas frees Hawkeye.

This man is a friend of the Delaware!

The hour is nigh![4] Uncas is found!

These Yengeese are my prisoners.

You have no claim over those who escaped from you.

The dark-haired one did not escape!

Then take her!

The Delaware will pay for their treachery!

The dark-haired woman must not be left to the savagery of Magua.

The Delaware will aid you against the Huron.

1. tongue: language.   2. trial by fire: a test of bravery that used physical pain or torture.
3. Great Turtle: There were three clans (family groups) within the Mohican tribe – Wolf, Turkey, and Turtle or Tortoise. Uncas's tattoo shows that he is descended from a great leader, and so Uncas is considered to be someone that deserves honor and respect.
4. The hour is nigh!: The time has come!

36

Uncas leads 200 Delaware braves[1] against the Huron village.

Hawkeye leads a smaller force, hoping to flank the enemy.[2]

As Hawkeye reaches the beaver meadow, the Hurons open fire!

BANG!

Killdeer finds its mark repeatedly but the Delaware are outnumbered.

CRACK!

BANG!

Suddenly Uncas appears with the main force, driving the Hurons back.

BANG!

The Huron village is overrun by Uncas and the Delaware. Magua realizes he is defeated.

But the Huron will not give up his prize.

Cora!

Argh!

Uncas fights through a group of Huron warriors and gives chase.

I will go no further. Kill me or set me free!

Reaching a cliff near the cavern, Cora struggles to escape from Magua.

1. braves: Native American warriors.   2. flank the enemy: surprise the enemy by attacking them from the side.

THE FINAL STRUGGLE

As Uncas appears, Magua holds a knife to Cora's throat.

Choose, Cora: live as my wife — or die!

Uncas hits Magua, but another Huron kills Cora.

Uncas attacks Cora's killer.

But Magua is quickly on his feet.

Argh!

As Uncas falls, Hawkeye and Duncan appear.

Hawkeye shoots . . .

. . . but Magua fatally stabs Uncas . . .

. . . and Hawkeye's bullet finds its target too late.

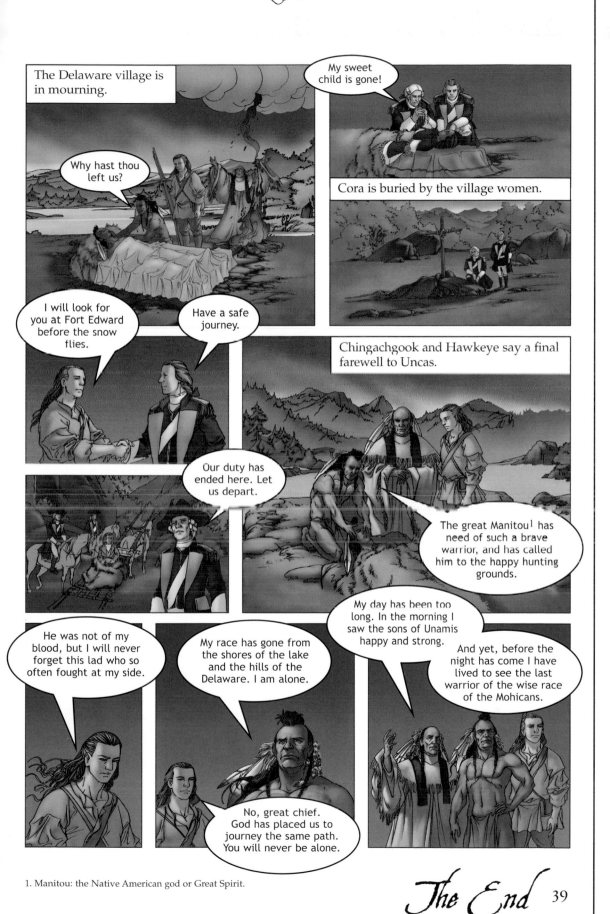

1. Manitou: the Native American god or Great Spirit.

The End 39

James Fenimore Cooper, author of thirty-four historical novels, was the first American writer to earn international recognition. His most famous books, the five-volume *Leatherstocking* series, tell the story of Natty Bumppo, a hunter and woodsman known as Hawkeye or Leatherstocking. Cooper also wrote several short stories, as well as books on his political views, and *Gleanings in Europe*, a four-volume description of his European travels. He wrote the first American sea novel, *The Pilot*, in 1824, the first American fiction trilogy, *The Littlepage Manuscripts*, in 1845–1846, and the first history of the American navy in 1839.

An engraving of James Fenimore Cooper, 1831.

EARLY LIFE

Cooper was born in Burlington, New Jersey, the eleventh child of Quaker parents, William and Elizabeth (Fenimore) Cooper. William Cooper was a judge who served in Congress (U.S. government). When James was a year old his father moved the family to upstate New York and founded the village of Cooperstown, which today forms part of the town of Otsego. Young James grew up on the shores of Otsego Lake, listening to tales of early settlers and roaming the forests which played a large part in many of his writings.

James enrolled at Yale College at the age of 14, but he was expelled for playing pranks. At 17 he joined the navy, and served for five years, reaching the rank of midshipman. When his father died in 1811, Cooper resigned and returned to Cooperstown.

That year he married Susan DeLancey, whose family owned large tracts of land in upstate New York.

COOPER THE WRITER

Cooper's first novel, *Precaution*, was published in 1821, but it was *The Spy* (1822) that established his reputation as a writer. The next year he published *The Pioneers*, the first of the *Leatherstocking Tales*. The second book in the series, *The Last of the Mohicans*, which appeared in 1826, is perhaps his best-known work and was widely read in Europe as well as the United States. Although his books were published in several languages (English, French, and German), Cooper suffered several financial setbacks and was in debt most of his later life.

POLITICAL CAREER

James Fenimore Cooper moved to France in 1826, serving there as U.S. Consul (an official U.S. representative in Paris) until 1833. During this time he continued to write extensively, publishing eight novels and several short stories and the political essay "Letter to General Lafayette." On his return to the U.S. he began work on *A Letter to His Countrymen*, a criticism of American culture that was poorly received.

THE AMERICAN WILDERNESS

As one of the first major American writers, Cooper helped to create a sense of nationalism in the early U.S. Republic, painting a romantic view of American history and the pioneer spirit. His writing established the popular images of the American frontier that became prominent in literature, and later in movies and television. But his work was more appreciated in Europe than in the United States.

A key theme in the *Leatherstocking Tales* is the conflict between the Native American tribes and white settlers along the frontier. While Cooper is sympathetic to the Indians, he portrays them in a way that was fashionable at the time, as "noble savages."

CULTURAL CONFLICTS

Cooper lived in a dynamic time in American history – a time of tension between settlers and the Native Americans being forced off of their lands. American settlers seeking a national identity sought at various times to preserve the traditions of the Indian tribes, while playing down the fact that the settlement of North America required the removal of the Native Americans.

Cooper's writing reflects this double standard – celebrating the advance of American culture while mourning the loss of the Indian way of life. This view extends to his portrayal of the Native Americans, whom he respects for their ability to live in harmony with nature even as he finds them to be backward, childlike, and brutal. Hawkeye's views on Native American tribes are the same as Cooper's – to him, the Mohicans are honorable, while the Hurons are ruthless and savage.

CRITICISM AND PRAISE

Some American writers have poked fun at Cooper's elaborate style. Mark Twain wrote "Fenimore Cooper's Literary Offenses" in 1895, in which he describes Cooper's writing as "destitute," having no "order, system, sequence, or result." The poet James Russell Lowell described Cooper's depiction of women as "sappy," and "flat as a prairie." Yet, Cooper was considered to be a brilliant writer by many of his contemporaries, such as French novelist Victor Hugo, who declared James Fenimore Cooper to be "the great master of modern romance." Years later, D. H. Lawrence would refer to the *Leatherstocking Tales* as a "crescendo of beauty."

Cooper enjoyed international success in his lifetime. He died on September 14, 1851, and is buried in Cooperstown, New York, but his writing is still celebrated today.

THE FRENCH AND INDIAN WAR

"THE WAR THAT MADE AMERICA"

During the 1700s, France and England fought a series of wars over land in European-controlled parts of North America. The last of these, the French and Indian War (known in Europe as the Seven Years' War), is the setting for *The Last of the Mohicans*. But although the siege of Fort William Henry was a real historical event, most of the book's characters and storylines are fictional.

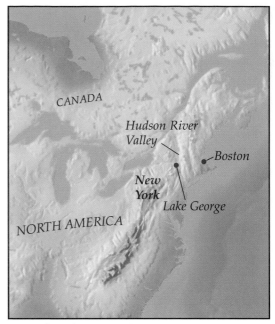

Map of northeast America.

PIONEERS

In the 1750s American settlers, or colonists, began crossing the Appalachian Mountains in search of good farmland in the Ohio River Valley. The French, who had colonized Canada as early as 1605, claimed this territory and resented American efforts to settle on land that they believed belonged to the king of France.

In July 1754, a Virginian army led by George Washington encountered French soldiers near Fort Duquesne (modern-day Pittsburg, Pennsylvania). After a short battle Colonel Washington was forced to surrender. For the next nine years American colonists, supported by the English army, would fight the French and their Native American allies. In 1756, England declared war on France, extending the struggle to Europe, India, and the sugar islands of the West Indies.

FORTIFICATIONS

There were no roads through the wilderness that separated French Canada from the British North American colonies. Instead, the Hudson River Valley, Lake Champlain, Lake George, and the Mohawk River Valley were major routes for both armies along the frontier. In 1755 the British built two forts north of Albany, New York – Fort Edward on the Hudson River and Fort William Henry a few miles north on the south shore of Lake George. In response, the French built Fort Carillon (later renamed Ticonderoga by the British) on the north shore of Lake George and used this fortification to launch an attack against Fort William Henry in the summer of 1757.

THE "MASSACRE"

The siege of Fort William Henry only lasted a week before Lieutenant Colonel George Munro was forced to surrender. The fort was destroyed by the French after it had been evacuated, but the accounts of the "massacre" that Cooper portrays in *The Last of the Mohicans* are sketchy, with casualties ranging from less than thirty people to over 500.

The next year (1758), the British retaliated and launched a major attack on Fort Carillon with an army of 16,000, but could not overcome the fort which had only about 4,000 defenders. A few months later the British were victorious in their attack on Louisbourg, a French fortification on Cape Breton Island that controlled access to the St. Lawrence River. Later that year the British captured Fort Duquesne, renaming it Fort Pitt after Prime Minister William Pitt.

THE END OF THE WAR

In the summer of 1759, the British captured Fort Niagara on Lake Ontario and renewed their attack on Fort Carillon, which the French eventually abandoned. A few months later British forces led by General James Wolfe captured the fortress at Quebec, and the next year Montreal surrendered, effectively ending the war in North America.

The Treaty of Paris of 1763 gave the English control of all French lands in Canada as well as the Ohio and Mississippi Rivers. The New York forts would become important again in the American Revolution in the 1770s, and the English would use their base in Canada to invade the Hudson River Valley – much as the French had done during the French and Indian War.

Map showing the area around Fort William Henry at the time of the siege.

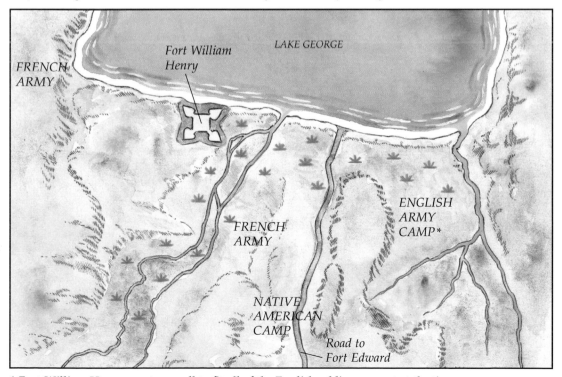

* *Fort William Henry was too small to fit all of the English soldiers present at the time of the siege, so a camp was set up to house the extra men.*

"Few men exhibit greater diversity . . . of character than the native warrior of North America. In war, he is daring, boastful, cunning, ruthless, self-denying, and self-devoted; in peace, just, generous, hospitable, revengeful, superstitious, modest, and commonly chaste."

> The Last of the Mohicans

James Fenimore Cooper was born in 1789, the year that George Washington was sworn in as the first president of the United States. Cooper grew up during the first decade of the nineteenth century – a time marked by rapid population growth and economic expansion. American colonists also established the Northwest Territories – the future states of Ohio, Indiana, Michigan, Illinois, and Wisconsin. With the purchase of the Louisiana Territory in 1803, the United States doubled in size, extending the American frontier to the Rocky Mountains and beyond.

U.S. PROGRESS

Like many young people of his generation, Cooper believed the United States was a nation that was destined to settle and "civilize" the American continent "from sea to shining sea." His novels reflect the interwoven themes of the natural beauty of the wilderness, the advancement of colonial ideas and culture, the heroic quality of the American woodsman, and the gradual defeat and disappearance of the Indian tribes.

"Give me the range!" said Hawk-eye, bending to catch a glimpse of the direction, and then instantly moving onward."

Last of the Mohicans. p. 72.

Hawkeye and Uncas find a track, while their party looks on apprehensively. Taken from an 1872 edition of The Last of the Mohicans.

ROMANTIC NOVELS

Cooper's writing conveys the ideals of American nationalism, as well as the romantic ideas that marked the literature, art, and music of the early nineteenth century. Cooper's writings embody the common traits of romantic novels – exotic settings, nature as an untamed force, rugged self-reliance, and a hero whose selflessness and bravery are unmatched.

The character of Hawkeye is based on one or more of the older woodsmen who were living in or around Cooperstown in the early years of settlement, and Cooper's romantic, if narrow, portrayal of Native Americans (as reflected in the quote above) is likely based on the stories he heard as a

young boy. Other influences on his writing include real-life woodsmen such as Daniel Boone, mountain men and fur trappers who explored the American West, as well as the success of the Lewis and Clark Expedition, which crossed the continent of North American in 1803–1806.

THE *LEATHERSTOCKING* SERIES

The five books of the *Leatherstocking* series are historical novels set between 1744 and 1804. The first novel, *The Pioneers, or The Sources of the Susquehanna, a Descriptive Tale*, is fourth chronologically in the series and introduces the reader to Natty Bumppo, known also as Hawkeye, the Deerslayer, the Pathfinder, Leatherstocking, and *La Longue Carabine*, or Long Rifle. The second book (the third chronologically),

The Last of the Mohicans, or A Narrative of 1757, tells the story of the massacre at Fort William Henry. The third novel, *The Prairie: A Tale* (last in the series chronologically), follows Natty Bumppo as he heads west in search of a new wilderness in Nebraska. The fourth book (second in the series), *The Pathfinder, or The Inland Sea*, is a tale of love and betrayal that is also set in the French and Indian War. The final offering, *The Deerslayer, or The First War Path*, is chronologically the first in the series and introduces a young Natty Bumppo and his lifelong friend, Chingachgook.

The Last of the Mohicans is Cooper's best-known novel, and the images of Hawkeye, Uncas, and Chingachgook have become part of American folklore and legend.

ONLINE RESOURCES

COOPER'S MAJOR WORKS

1820: *Precaution* – a novel set 1813–1814.

1821: *The Spy: A Tale on Neutral Ground* – a novel about the American Revolution.

1823: *The Pioneers, or The Sources of the Susquehanna* – first of the *Leatherstocking Tales*.

1823: *Tales of Fifteen, or Imagination and Heart* – two short stories published under the pseudonym of Jane Morgan.

1824: *The Pilot: A Tale of the Sea* – novel about naval fighter John Paul Jones.

1825: *Lionel Lincoln, or The Leaguer of Boston* – novel about the beginnings of the Revolutionary War.

1826: *The Last of the Mohicans, or A Narrative of 1757* – second *Leatherstocking Tale*, set during the French and Indian War.

1827: *The Prairie* – *Leatherstocking Tale* set in the Northwest Territories.

1828: *The Red Rover, A Tale* – pirate story set in 1759.

1828: *Notions of the Americans: Picked Up by a Traveling Bachelor* – a look at American life for European readers.

1830: *The Waterwitch, or The Skimmer of the Seas* – story of smugglers set in 1713 New York.

1830: *Letter to General Lafayette* – political treatise on the cost of government.

1832: *The Heidenmauer, or The Benedictines, a Legend of the Rhine* – set in 16th-century Germany.

1833: *The Headsman, or The Abbaye des Vignerons* – novel set in 18th-century Switzerland.

1836: "The Eclipse" – Cooper's experiences of an eclipse in Cooperstown, New York.

1837–1838: *Gleanings in Europe* – a description of Cooper's European travels.

1838: *Homeward Bound* – first of the Effingham novels, a romantic sea story.

1838: *Home Is Found* – second of the Effingham novels.

1840: *The Pathfinder, or The Inland Sea* – fourth *Leatherstocking Tale*.

1841: *The Deerslayer, or The First War Path* – last of the *Leatherstocking Tales*.

1843: *Wyandotte* – novel set in New York during the Revolutionary War.

1844: *Afloat and Ashore: A Sea Tale* – The story of a young man who runs away to sea in 1797.

1845: *Satanstoe, or The Littlepage Manuscripts: A Tale of the Colony* – first book of a trilogy about a New York family.

1845: *The Chainbearer* – second of *The Littlepage Manuscripts*.

1846: *The Redskins* – a third volume of *The Littlepage Manuscripts*.

1847: *The Crater, or Vulcan's Peak* – story of a doctor shipwrecked in the Pacific Ocean.

1848: *Oak Openings* – Native American story set in western Michigan during the War of 1812.

1849: *The Sea Lions* – tale of a sealing expedition set in 1819.

1850: *The Ways of the Hour* – Cooper's last full-length novel; a murder mystery to examine American society of the 1840s.

FILM AND TELEVISION

T he *Leatherstocking Tales* have inspired filmmakers since the very beginning of cinema history. The heroic stories of Hawkeye have been told to every generation, and Cooper's romantic images of the American wilderness and the "noble, savage" Indians have captured the imaginations of moviegoers in dozens of theatrical and television presentations.

Hawkeye and Uncas lead Major Heyward through the forest in The Last of the Mohicans, *1992.*

Leather Stocking, 1909, silent film by D. W. Griffith.

The Deerslayer, 1913, silent film starring Harry Morley as Hawkeye.

The Last of the Mohicans, 1920, silent film with Wallace Beery as Magua.

Leatherstocking, 1924, silent film starring Harold Miller as Hawkeye.

The Last of the Mohicans, 1932, with Harry Carey as Hawkeye.

The Last of the Mohicans, 1936, starring Randolph Scott as Hawkeye.

Drums Along the Mohawk, 1939, starring Henry Fonda as Hawkeye.

The Pioneers, 1941, starring Tex Ritter and Slim Andrews.

Last of the Redmen, 1947, starring Jon Hall as Major Duncan Heyward and Buster Crabbe as Magua, adapted from *The Last of the Mohicans*.

The Iroquois Trail, 1950: Hawkeye, played by George Montgomery, aids the British during the French and Indian War.

The Pathfinder, 1952, starring George Montgomery as the Pathfinder (Hawkeye).

The Deerslayer, 1957, starring Lex Barker as Hawkeye.

Hawkeye and the Last of the Mohicans, 1957, television series starring Jon Hart as Hawkeye and Lon Chaney Jr. as Chingachgook.

The Last of the Mohicans, 1971, television miniseries.

The Last of the Mohicans, 1975, animated movie starring John Doucette as the voice of Chingachgook.

The Last of the Mohicans, 1977, television movie starring Steve Forrest.

The Last of the Mohicans, 1987, animated television series starring Jon Waters.

The Last of the Mohicans, 1992, with Daniel Day Lewis as Hawkeye, Wes Studi as Magua, and Russell Means as Chingachgook.

INDEX

A
adaptations 47
Albany 42

C
Chingachgook 45
Cooper, Elizabeth
  (Fenimore) 40
Cooper, James
  Fenimore 40–41
    influences 44–45
    works 46
Cooper, William 40
Cooperstown 40, 44

D
The Deerslayer 45, 46

F
films 47
Forts
  Carillon 42, 43

Duquesne 42, 43
Edward 42
Niagara 42
William Henry 42, 45
French and Indian War
  42–43, 45

H
Hawkeye 40, 44–45, 47
Hudson River Valley 42

L
Last of the Mohicans
  41, 44–45, 46
Leatherstocking Tales
  40–41, 44–45, 46
*Letter to General
  Lafayette* 41, 42, 46

N
Northwest Territories
  44

O
Ohio River Valley 42, 43
Otsego 40

P
The Pathfinder 45, 46
The Pioneers 41, 45, 46
Precaution 41, 46

R
romantic novels 44

S
The Spy 41, 46

U
Uncas 44, 45

W
Washington, George
  42, 44

IF YOU ENJOYED THIS BOOK, YOU MIGHT LIKE TO TRY
THESE OTHER TITLES IN BARRON'S *GRAPHIC CLASSICS* SERIES:

Adventures of Huckleberry Finn
  Mark Twain

Dr. Jekyll and Mr. Hyde
  Robert Louis Stevenson

Dracula Bram Stoker

Frankenstein Mary Shelley

Gulliver's Travels Jonathan Swift

Hamlet William Shakespeare

The Hunchback of Notre Dame Victor Hugo

Jane Eyre Charlotte Brontë

Journey to the Center of the Earth
  Jules Verne

Julius Caesar William Shakespeare

Kidnapped Robert Louis Stevenson

Macbeth William Shakespeare

The Merchant of Venice
  William Shakespeare

The Man in the Iron Mask
  Alexandre Dumas

Moby Dick Herman Melville

The Odyssey Homer

Oliver Twist Charles Dickens

Romeo and Juliet William Shakespeare

A Tale of Two Cities Charles Dickens

The Three Musketeers Alexandre Dumas

Treasure Island Robert Louis Stevenson

20,000 Leagues Under the Sea Jules Verne

Wuthering Heights Emily Brontë